Beautiful Crooked Letter I

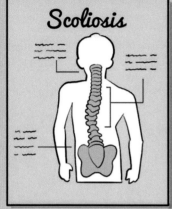

Scoliosis

by Shae Smith

Illustrations by
Mike Motz

This book is dedicated to all scoliosis warriors.
Be strong, be brave, and be YOU!

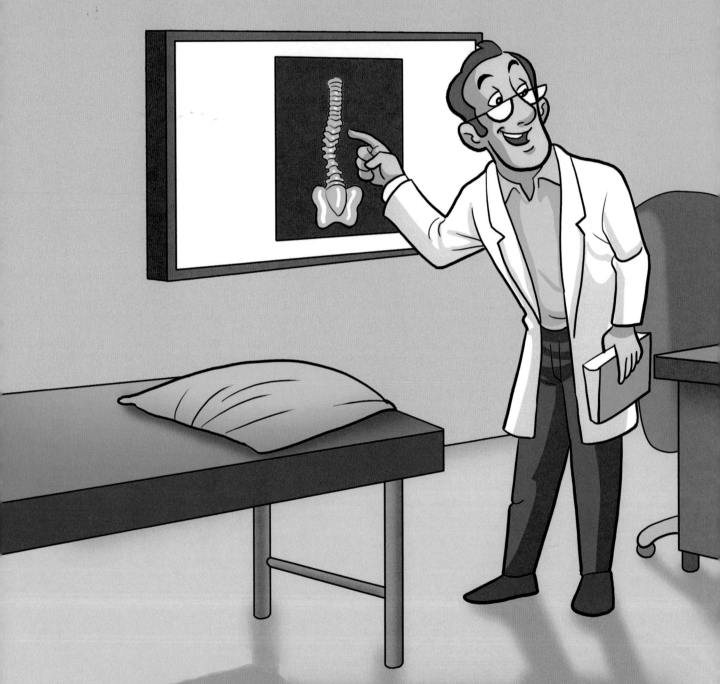

Beautiful Crooked Letter I

by Shae Smith

Illustrations by
Mike Motz

It was the first day of school, and Izzy was excited to see all of her friends. They had so many stories to tell, but the bell rang.

The principal announced over the intercom
that students will be checked today
for scoliosis during PE class.

"What is scoliosis?" asked Izzy.

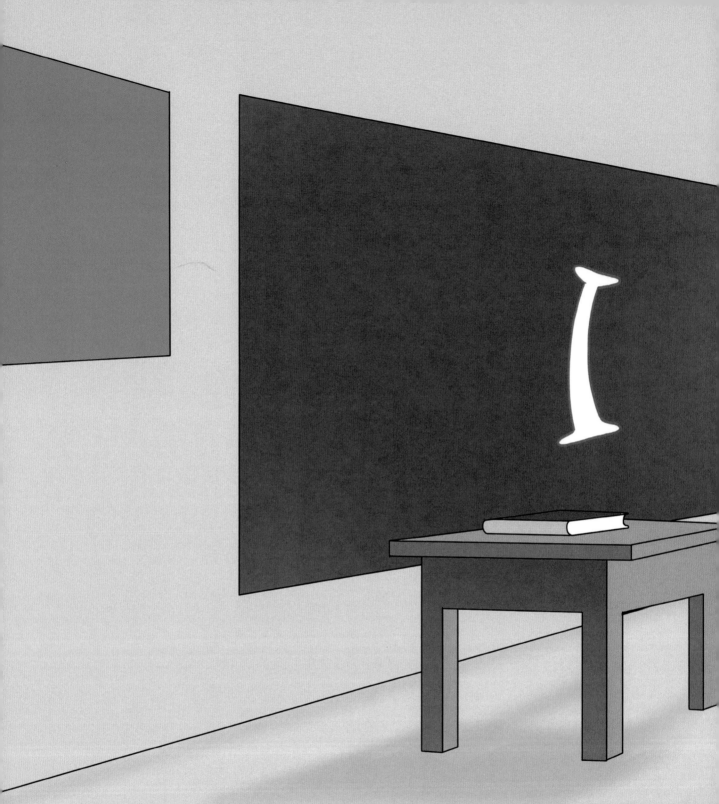

Mrs. Smith explained to the class that scoliosis is when the backbone is not straight but bends either to the right or to the left. She said, "It is like a crooked letter 'I'."

During PE class, the nurse called each student one by one in a room and shut the door. "What could they be doing in there?" Izzy asked her friend Hope.

Hope shrugged her shoulders.

It was Izzy's turn to walk to the room.
Behind the door she was asked to bend over
and keep her hands together.
The nurse looked at her back, touched her back,
and then told her to stand up.
She was free to go back to PE class.

Izzy and her friends talked about how easy that was and went back to sharing their summer stories.

Izzy bounced off the school bus and ran into her house, excited about her first day of school. Her mom, Sarah, listened to every word.

Her mom then told her she had something to share with her. "The school nurse called today and encouraged me to take you to a doctor. They think you may have scoliosis," said Sarah.

Izzy was confused and couldn't sleep that night.

The next day Sarah and Izzy waited patiently at Dr. Dan's office. So many questions were going through Izzy's mind.

Dr. Dan shared with Izzy that her x-ray showed a curve in her backbone, but it was good that she caught the curve early. However, all Izzy could think was that she had a crooked letter "I."

Izzy's friends learned that she had scoliosis,
and they started asking a lot of questions at school.

Some kids even started calling her "crooked Izzy."
This made her sad.

Izzy continued to hide her back at school.
She wore big clothes, started sitting in the corner,
and quit talking to her friends.

Her friend Hope was really worried about her.

Hope decided to talk to Izzy. She told her that she thought Izzy was beautiful, smart, funny, and she could still kick a ball harder than the boys. She even held the shuttle run record, and nothing would change that.

Hope continued to tell her that she may be crooked,
but she was beautifully crooked and she was strong.

Izzy didn't feel strong because she cried and she was scared. She had so many emotions and didn't know what to do, but she thought about what Hope had said. Her friend thought she was beautiful, smart, funny, AND strong.

Being crooked was something to add to that list, and it was something only Izzy herself could be. She finally realized how unique she was, and it wasn't a bad thing.

It was Monday, and Izzy walked into school with a new smile and a new spaghetti strap dress. She was no longer scared to let others see her back.

Izzy was a beautiful crooked letter "I" and proud of it! The things that made her different were the things that made her Izzy.

About the Author

Shae Smith is a high school student in Bolivar, Missouri, and an advocate for scoliosis awareness. She is a devoted student, competitive dancer, and Outstanding Teen title holder using her own journey with scoliosis to inspire others. Shae has created a website, catchingthecurve.com, organized the "Confidently Curvy" fashion show, and proclaimed September 1 as Scoliosis Awareness Day in the state of MO with official signing by Missouri's governor.

Shae is highly involved with local charities including Children's Miracle Network Hospitals, Ronald McDonald House, Trisomy 18 Foundation, Salvation Army, Crooked Life Foundation, and the National Scoliosis Foundation. Shae is also the recipient of the Miss Missouri Outstanding Teen program's Cindy Baker Community Scholarship Award, the Outstanding Youth Philanthropist of the Year Award, Children Miracle Network's Miracle Maker Award, and Miss America Serves Top National Individual Fundraiser raising to date approximately $29,000.

53153899R00018